Seeing Red

Robert Munsch

illustrated by
Michael Martchenko

Scholastic Canada Ltd.
New York Toronto London Auckland Sydney
Mexico City New Delhi Hong Kong Buenos Aires

Scholastic Canada Ltd.
604 King Street West, Toronto, Ontario M5V 1E1, Canada

Scholastic Inc.
557 Broadway, New York, NY 10012, USA

Scholastic Australia Pty Limited
PO Box 579, Gosford, NSW 2250, Australia

Scholastic New Zealand Limited
Private Bag 94407, Botany, Manukau 2163, New Zealand

Scholastic Children's Books
Euston House, 24 Eversholt Street, London NW1 1DB, UK

www.scholastic.ca

The illustrations in this book were painted in watercolour
on Crescent illustration board.
The type is set in 21 point ITC Clearface.

Library and Archives Canada Cataloguing in Publication
Munsch, Robert N., 1945-
Seeing red / by Robert Munsch ; illustrated by Michael Martchenko.
ISBN 978-1-4431-2446-1
I. Martchenko, Michael II. Title.
PS8576.U575S44 2013a   jC813'.54   C2012-906431-9

6 5 4 3 2 1   Printed in Canada 119   13 14 15 16 17

*For Arie Baazov,
Montreal, Quebec.
– R.M.*

"Arie," said Alex, "your hair is fantastic! You are the only kid in the whole school with red hair! What is the secret?"

"Well," said Arie, "it really IS a secret and I am NOT supposed to tell anyone, but I will tell you because you are my best friend.

"I was not born with red hair. I turned it red by eating tomatoes. Lots of tomatoes! I eat ten big, red tomatoes for breakfast every day."

The next morning Alex ate ten big, red tomatoes for breakfast:

1 ^{2} 3 $_4$ 5 ^{6} 7 $_8$ 9 ^{10}

Then he ran to the bathroom to look at his hair in the mirror.
It was still black.

Alex ran to Arie's house and yelled,
"Look at my HAIR, Arie!
"It is still BLACK, Arie!
"What is going on, Arie?
"What is GOING ON?"

"OH!" said Arie. "I forgot about the ketchup. How could I forget about the ketchup? You have to drink a large bottle of red ketchup after you eat the tomatoes."

"Right," said Alex. "That makes a lot of sense. I should have thought of that."

The next day for breakfast Alex ate ten big, red tomatoes:

1 2 3 4 5 6 7 8 9 10

drank a large bottle of red ketchup:

GLUG GLUG GLUG GLUG GLUG GLUG GLUG

and was almost sick — GWACKH!

Then Alex ran to a mirror and looked at his hair.
It was still black.

He ran to Arie's house and yelled,
"Look at my HAIR, Arie!
"It is still BLACK, Arie!
"What is going on, Arie?
"What is GOING ON?"

"Let me think," said Arie. "OH! I forgot the most important thing! After the tomatoes and ketchup, you have to drink a bottle of Very Red, Very Hot, Mexican Pepper Sauce. It sets the colour."

"That makes a lot of sense," said Alex. "I should have thought of that myself."

The next day Alex ate ten big, red tomatoes:

1 ^{2} 3 $_4$ 5 ^{6} 7 $_8$ 9 ^{10}

drank a large bottle of red ketchup:

GLUG GLUG GLUG GLUG GLUG GLUG GLUG

and was almost sick — GWACKH!

Then he started to drink a bottle of Very Red, Very Hot, Mexican Pepper Sauce.

GLUG GLUG GLUG GLUG . . .

**"AAAAHHHHHH!
AAAAHHHHHH!
AAAAHHHHHHH!"**

GREEN smoke came out of one ear, RED smoke came out of his other ear, and FIRE came out of his nose.

Alex ran into the kitchen and put his head under the faucet until the steam stopped coming out of his nose, and then he said, "I think Arie is fooling me! Well, I am going to fool Arie!"

Alex went to school and said, "Hey, Arie! It worked! It worked! It worked! My hair turned red! But I didn't like my hair red, so I changed it back to black."

"WOW!" said Arie. "How did you do that?"

"Easy!" said Alex. "I ate ten long pieces of black licorice."

On the way home, Arie bought ten long pieces of black licorice and ate them:

$$1 \quad {}^{2} \quad 3 \quad {}_{4} \quad 5 \quad {}^{6} \quad 7 \quad {}_{8} \quad 9 \quad {}^{10}$$

Then he ran to the bathroom and looked at his hair in the mirror. It was still red.

He ran to Alex's house and yelled,

"Look at my HAIR, Alex!

"It is still RED, Alex!

"What is going on, Alex?

"What is GOING ON?"

"OH!" said Alex. "I forgot about the coffee. You have to grab a cup of your dad's black coffee and drink the whole thing."

"Right," said Arie. "That makes a lot of sense. I should have thought of that."

So Arie went home and ate ten more long pieces of black licorice:

1 ^{2} 3 $_4$ 5 ^{6} 7 $_8$ 9 ^{10}

drank a large cup of his dad's black coffee:

GLUG GLUG GLUG GLUG GLUG GLUG GLUG

and was almost sick — GWACKH!

Then he ran to a mirror and looked at his hair. It was still red!

Arie ran to Alex's house and yelled,
"Look at my HAIR, Alex!
"It is still RED, Alex!
"What is going on, Alex?
"What is GOING ON?"

"Let me think," said Alex. "OH! I forgot the most important thing! After the licorice and coffee, you have to eat a whole box of black pepper. It sets the colour."

"Right," said Arie. "That makes a lot of sense. I should have thought of that."

So Arie went home and ate ten long pieces of black licorice:

$$1 \quad {}^{2} \quad 3 \quad {}_{4} \quad 5 \quad {}^{6} \quad 7 \quad {}_{8} \quad 9 \quad {}^{10}$$

drank a large cup of his dad's black coffee:

GLUG GLUG GLUG GLUG GLUG GLUG GLUG

and was almost sick — GWACKH!

Then Arie ate a whole box of black pepper:

CHOMP CHOMP CHOMP CHOMP . . .

Robert Munsch

Seeing Red

illustrated by
Michael Martchenko

New!

SCHOLASTIC

"AAAAHHHHHHH!

AAAAHHHHHHH!

AAAAHHHHHHH!"

GREEN smoke came out of one ear, RED smoke came out of the other ear, and FIRE came out of his nose.

Arie put his head under the kitchen faucet until the steam stopped coming out of his nose.

"Ha!" he said. "Alex fooled me, too!"

He ran to Alex's house and said, "I know how our hair can be the same . . ."

"Let's both make it purple!"